For my mum. You always told me "to keep on trying".
At least, that's what I thought you said...

First published 2013 by Walker Books Ltd, 87 Vauxhall Walk, London SE11 5HJ • 10 9 8 7 6 5 4 3 2 1
• © 2013 Andy Pritchett • The right of Andy Pritchett to be identified as author/illustrator of this work has
been asserted by him in accordance with the Copyright, Designs and Patents Act 1988 • This book has been
typeset in Imperfect Bold, Cooper Five Opti Black, Countryhouse, Goudy Stout and Kosmic • Printed in China
• All rights reserved. No part of this book may be reproduced, transmitted or stored in an information retrieval
system in any form or by any means, graphic, electronic or mechanical, including photocopying, taping and
recording, without prior written permission from the publisher. • British Library Cataloguing in Publication Data: a
catalogue record for this book is available from the British Library • ISBN 978-1-4063-4034-1 • www.walker.co.uk

STICK!

Andy Pritchett

WALKER BOOKS

AND SUBSIDIARIES

LONDON · BOSTON · SYDNEY · AUCKLAND

Worm!

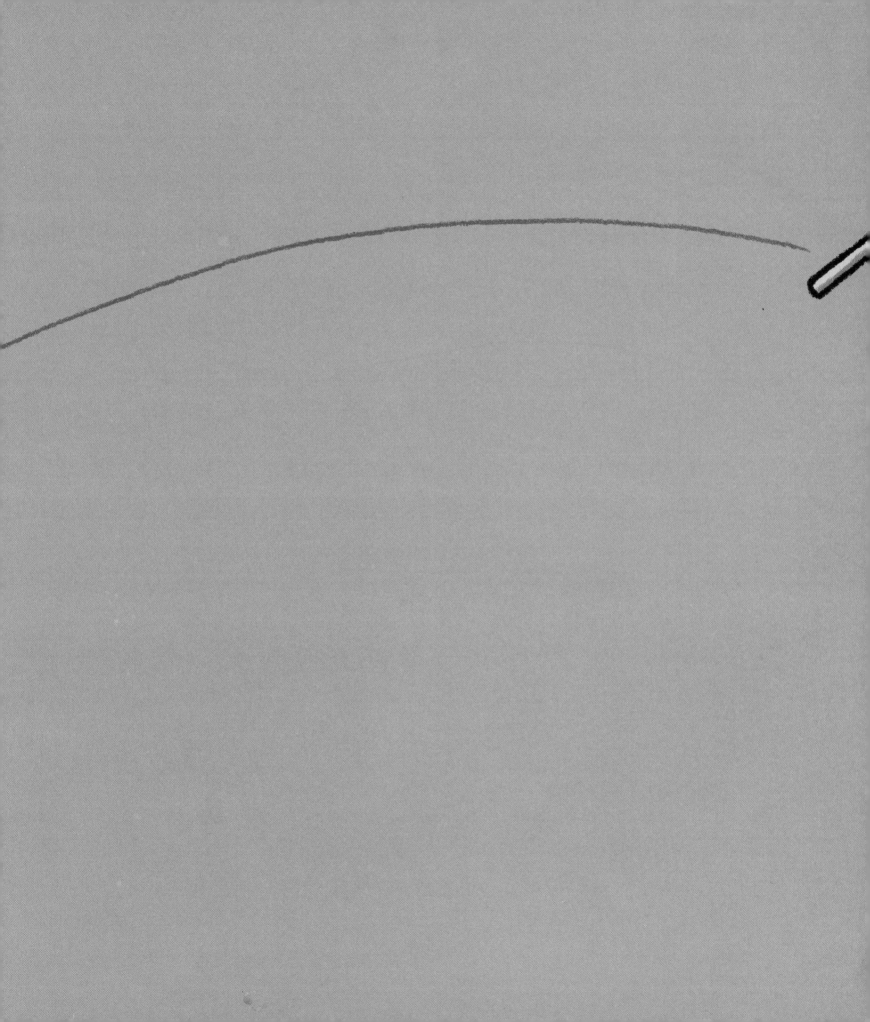

CLUNK!

Friend?